Frog Wars

By Cindy Kenney and Doug Peterson
Illustrated by Michael Moore

veggietales.com

.com

ZONDERKIDZ

Frog Wars
© 2005 Big Idea, Inc. VEGGIETALES®, character names, likenesses and other indicia are
trademarks of Big Idea, Inc. All rights reserved.

Requests for information should be addressed to:
Zonderkidz, *Grand Rapids, Michigan* 49530

ISBN 978-0-310-70627-4

Written by: Cindy Kenney & Doug Peterson
Illustrated by: Michael Moore
Editor: Cindy Kenney
Art Direction & Design: Karen Poth

Printed in Hong Kong

12 13 14 15 16 17 /PEH/ 21 20 19 18 17 16

"Be strong, all you who put your hope in the Lord.
Never give up."

(Psalm 31:24)

Junior Asparagus had been trying to learn how to play the tuba all day. But the noise coming out of it sounded like a sick water buffalo with a pail on its head. **BWOOOOOOOOMBABLUUUURRRTT–BLATT!!!** echoed through the house.

Fifteen Minutes Later...

Junior slammed his tuba on the floor.

"I quit!" he shouted as his mom rushed into the room.

"Junior, you love music. And this is the fourth instrument you've tried this month," she said.

"Ya, but I'm no good at it," he puffed.

"Perhaps it's because you're using The **Advanced** Guide to Playing Tubas on your first day. Even if God made you musically gifted, it takes perseverance before you can play well."

"Percy-fear-ants? God never gave them to me."

"Perseverance means 'keep trying; don't give up hope.'"

"Hope?" he muttered. "Nope. Don't got it."

Later That Afternoon...

Junior wandered into the Treasure Trove Bookstore.

"Do you have any books on how to play the violin?" he asked Mr. O'Malley, the Irish potato who owned the store.

Mr. O'Malley peered at Junior. "I thought you were learning to play the tuba, laddie."

"Apparently, tubas and I weren't made for each other."

Mr. O'Malley's eyes lit up. "I have the perfect book for you."

O'Malley climbed a tall ladder to find the book.
"It's somewhere in the *Never-Say-Die* section, next to the Self-Help Comic
Books." Finally, he found it: *Frog Wars*.

Junior opened the book and saw a beautiful palace in the middle of a
desert. Workers lifted giant statues that looked like huge stone frogs.

At That Very Moment...

Four giant words floated up from the first page of the book.
Four simple words: **ONCE UPON A TIME.**

The four giant words swirled around Junior, and...
WHOOOOOOOOOOOOOOOOOOOSH!
Junior slid **down**
      down
          down.
But as he slid down the giant page, the words moved up!
They said: **A long time ago, in a land far, far away . . .**

EPISODE IV:
A REALLY, REALLY NEW HOPE
Dark Visor and his evil empire are
forcing the people of Salon to be
his slaves. He's making them build temples
to the great frog god, Ribbit. But the one
true God is rising up a hero to rescue them...

After sliding down the words, Junior crash-landed inside the *Frog Wars* book!

"Where did you come from?" asked a cucumber slave, hopping up to Junior.

"He fell from outer space," said a blueberry. "Hello, Space Boy. I'm Princess Hair-Spraya, and this is Cuke Sandwalker."

Junior stared at the cucumber's wig. Then he looked at Princess Hair-Spraya with a baffled look on his face. "You have cinnamon buns on your ears."

"Where else do you suggest I carry them?" she frowned. "I don't have hands, you know."

"Don't worry, we won't hurt you. We were captured from Salon, which is on the other side of the Big Frog Pond. We were brought here to be Dark Visor's slaves," the cucumber explained.

Just then, two other slaves peeked out from behind a frog statue. "Is it safe to come out, Master Cuke?" asked a pea dressed in gold.

"C'mon out," Cuke Sandwalker called.

The two peas cautiously approached the little asparagus. "I'm Sweet-Pea-3-Oh," said one of the peas. "This is Achoo Bless-U. We're slaves, too."

"Are you the one who's come to free our people?" asked Princess Hair-Spraya.

"I don't think so," said Junior, a little confused.

"We've been asking the one, true God to send someone who will lead us out of here. You *must* be the one!" said Cuke Sandwalker. "Follow us, Space Boy."

Junior stayed close behind as Cuke and his friends rushed through the palace and into the throne room.

The king, a zucchini named Dark Visor, sat on a great frog throne. His visor made his breathing sound funny.

"He hates the sunlight," whispered Achoo Bless-U.

"What's with all the frogs?" Junior asked.

"Dark Visor believes in a frog god called Ribbit," Princess Hair-Spraya told him. "He doesn't believe the true God will send someone to help us."

"So go ahead and tell him," nudged Cuke.

"Tell him what?" asked Junior.

"Tell him to let God's people go free!"

Trembling With Fear...

Junior moved toward the king.

"What do you want?" Dark Visor bellowed after lifting his visor.

"Let the people of Salon go free," Junior squeaked.

"NO!" thundered the king so loudly it caused his visor to slam shut.

"Okay, I gave it a shot," Junior shrugged and turned to leave.

"Wait!" said Cuke Sandwalker. "You hardly tried at all!"

"Trying isn't really my thing," Junior added as he ran for the door.

At That Very Moment...

. . . a guy named Mo stormed into the room carrying a walking stick. The big round tomato was on a mission.

"Stick with me," Mo told Junior. "We won't give up until Dark Visor gives in." Mo turned to the king and spoke. "My name is Mo! And God wants you to let his people go!"

But Dark Visor only snarled at him with a heavy breath.

"**Whmmmimmtwyouttodsiiiiiiii**."

"Huh?" everyone gasped.

"Lift your visor, and try it again," suggested Sweet-Pea-3-Oh.

The king flung his head back to open the visor and roared, "When I'm through with you, you will all turn to the dark side!"

Dark Visor would not let the slaves go free. But did Mo give up? Nope! He had hope and would not give up, because he put his faith in the Lord.

Mo warned Dark Visor that God would not be pleased, but the big zucchini didn't care. So Mo threatened to turn all the water in the kingdom to juice, and soon purple liquid bubbled from every drinking fountain in the city.

"This guy's really good," Cuke Sandwalker whispered to Junior.

Day After Day After Day...

Mo threatened the king with God's anger, but the king refused to let the people go. Junior just wanted to quit and go home.

But Mo encouraged him to stay. "God wants us to have faith in him. That means doing our best and *not* giving up," he told Junior. Then Mo shouted, "My name is Mo! And God wants you to let his people go!"

"No way, Jose," Dark Visor replied as he sipped his juice.

So the tomato warned the king that God would send plagues on the land. And plagues were scary things like...

...days and days of doing the Hokey Pokey.

...swarms of dust bunnies.

...a drought of pizza and ice cream.

...and the invasion of FROGS!

Even though the king worshiped the frog Ribbit, unwanted, *real* frogs turned up everywhere! The king found them in his cereal bowl. In his pajamas. Even on his throne! But Dark Visor would not let God's people go free.

Many Days Later...

"Isn't it time to give up?" asked Cuke Sandwalker.

"What do you think, Junior?" Mo asked.

Junior thought about it. *God wants us to put our hope in him and keep trying!*

"Anything else we can try?" Junior asked.

Mo smiled, and they prayed to God for help.

Then God sent a deep darkness to fall upon the land.

"Is this what you meant when you talked about turning to the dark side?"
Achoo Bless-U teased the king.

Finally...

...an amazing thing happened. Dark Visor heard that familiar voice... "My name is Mo! And God wants you to let his people go!"

"I can't see anything in the dark!" he groaned as he flipped his visor up just as he was about to sit on a frog. "Ribbit has turned against me in my time of need.

"Alright! Let the slaves go free, and take these frogs with you!" the king shouted.

The clouds began to part as the slaves marched out of the land. Junior rode in a wagon with his new friends, except there was no room for Cuke Sandwalker.

"Use the horse, Cuke!" said the princess.

"Good thinking," smiled the cucumber.

But Before the Slaves Could Get Away...

Dark Visor slammed down the lid of his visor and sent his army to chase after the slaves.

"**IchkabildGoafrtthslvsfslnan!**"

"Huh?"

He flipped his visor back open and shouted, "I changed my mind! Go after the slaves from Salon!"

The Empire struck back!

The slaves were trapped in front of the Big Frog Pond with no way to get across. In front of the slaves was the treacherous pond muck. The king's army was quickly approaching them. The people from Salon were afraid.

Junior was scared, too. But did he give up? Nope! He had hope! He saw how God continued to watch over the people again and again. He knew they had to trust God in a mighty way.

"Don't give up!" Junior shouted.

Then Mo called out: "You will see how the Lord will save you!"

Suddenly...

The lily pads in the pond came together and turned to stone while the waters parted to each side. God created a pathway so the slaves could get to the other side.

But Dark Visor's army was right behind them.

Did Junior and Mo give up?

Nope! They had hope!

As the Sun Began To Rise...

The slaves arrived on the other side of the pond, and the lily pads returned to normal. The pond filled with water and muck. The soldiers sank into tons of mud and water, and clamored to shore.

"It's not easy being mean," said the king, pulling himself out of the muck.

"Ribbit," said a frog behind him.

With the army defeated, the slaves cheered on the opposite shore.

And Then It Happened...

Two words suddenly popped out of the sand...along with several frogs. Two simple words: **THE END.**

"Thanks for not giving up, Junior!" said Mo.

"Thanks for teaching me to never give up!" replied Junior.

"Goodbye, Space Boy!" called Princess Hair-Spraya.

"Be strong and never lose hope," added Cuke Sandwalker. "May the Lord be with you."

The two giant words swirled around Junior like a desert whirlwind. The next thing Junior knew, he was back in the Treasure Trove Bookstore, shaking sand from his hat.

In the Store...

Mr. O'Malley shuffled out of the back room when he heard the bell above the door jingle.

Junior told Mr. O'Malley all about his adventure. Dark Visor. The frogs. Mo.

"Aye, but what did you learn?" asked Mr. O'Malley.

"That God wants us to have hope in him. And that we shouldn't give up, even when things get difficult," he said. "By the way, do you have *The **Beginner's** Guide to Playing Tubas?*"

"I sure do, laddie!" Mr. O'Malley chuckled. "Let it be my gift to you."

"Thanks!" Junior beamed as he hopped out of the store.

Then, Mr. O'Malley said to himself, *New hope you have. Happy that makes me.*

Want to read a real story about having hope in the Lord?
Read the story of Moses in Exodus, Chapters 1 to 15, in the Bible.